SAM PARROW BACK WHEN TIME STOOD STILL

Sam's 5th exciting time travel adventure

Gill Parkes

The nature of this book makes the appearance of certain biblical characters and events inevitable. All other characters and events portrayed in this book are fictitious and any similarity to real persons, living or dead, is coincidental and not intended by the author.
Scripture quotations are taken from the NIV translation and used with permission.

ISBN: 9798764733876
Imprint: Independently published

Cover design by: Art Painter
Library of Congress Control Number: 2018675309
Printed in the United States of America

To all my brothers and sisters in Christ at Beacon Church. May you always know your place in his kingdom and experience his presence in the storms of life.

"The Lord himself goes before you and will be with you; he will never leave you nor forsake you. Do not be afraid; do not be discouraged."

DEUTERONOMY CH 31 VS 8 NIV

CONTENTS

MAP OF ISRAEL

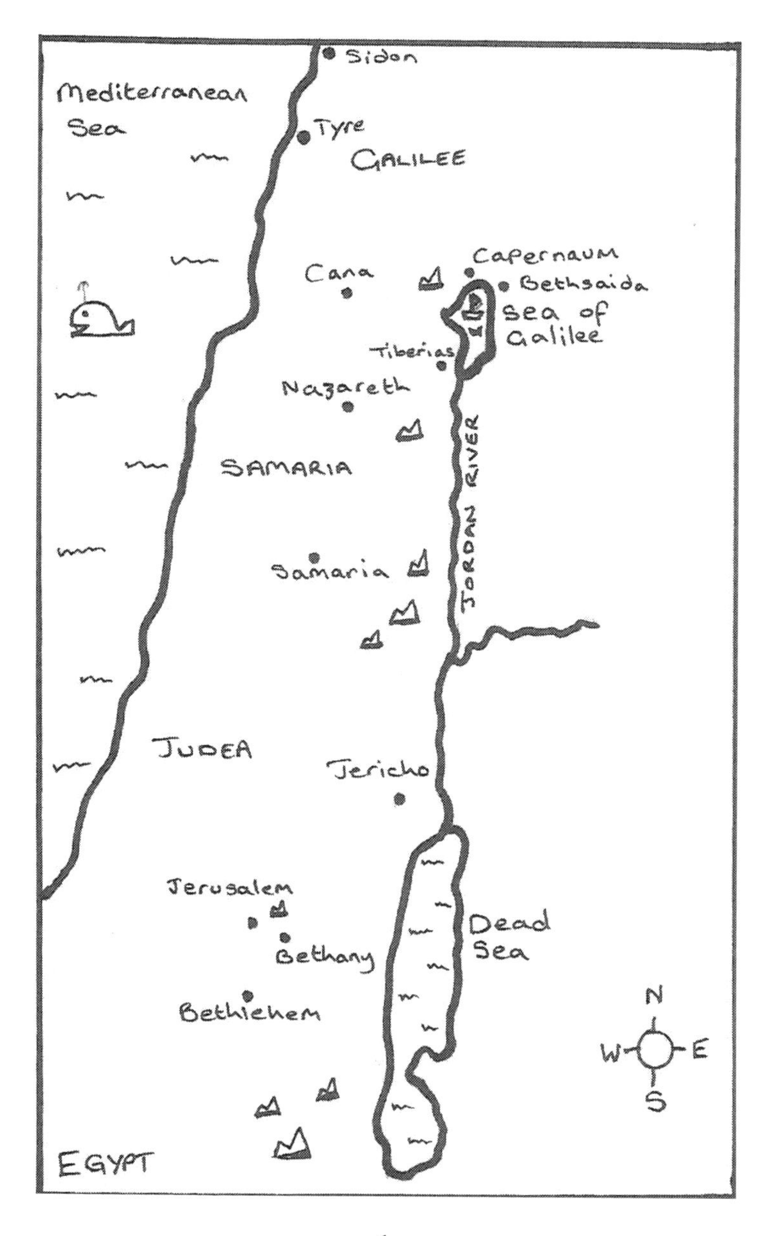

LIST OF CHARACTERS

Abraham, Isaac, Israel - *Ancestors, founding fathers of the Israelites*
Adah - *Rachel's daughter-in-law*
Ahab - *King of Israel*
Alex, Ben & Jamie - *Sam's friends, 21st Century*
Andy - *Sam's Dad*
Baal - *a false god*
Chris - *Youth group leader*
Daniel - *Advisor to King Nebuchadnezzar*
Eli & Jacob - *Rachel's brothers*
Elijah - *Prophet*
Hepzibah - *the goat*
Jesus - *Messiah*
Jezebel - *Ahab's wife*
Jo - *Sam's Mum*
Kate & Dayle - *Sisters, Sam's friends, 21st century*
Kieran - *Youth group member*
Matthew - *Sam's friend, 1st century*
Mr Stevens - *PE teacher*
Mrs Fletcher - *History teacher*
Nebuchadnezzar - *King of Babylon*
Ollie & Jack - *Year 7 bullies*
Rachel - *Sam's friend, 1st century*
Sam - *12-yr-old time traveller*

Sue Fielding/Peters - *Chris' wife*
Yahweh - *The One True God*

CHAPTER 1

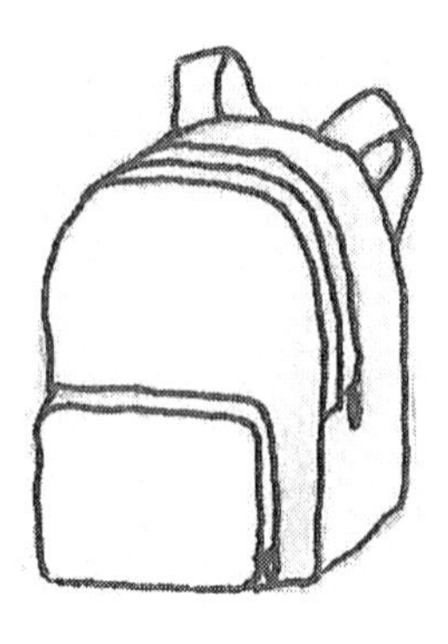

It had been hot and sticky all week. Even with all the windows open the air was still and had a heavy feeling, as though it was too weary to even raise enough energy to puff out a small breeze. A bee flew in through the window and buzzed around Sam's head, reminding him of his last adventure with the time stone when he spent four months on the ark. That had been the best trip ever! He hadn't liked it much afterwards though when he and Rachel had landed in Babel at the time the languages were all mixed up. Sam had panicked when he couldn't understand his friend, the thought of being stuck in ancient Israel and unable to ask for help was horrendous. It had all worked out okay though and the stone had taken him home the same time he had left – it had even given him a haircut!

As Sam's thoughts wandered back to his time travel journeys, his eyelids began to droop. Mrs Fletcher, the history teacher was talking to the class about the Magna Carta, some sort of contract King John was supposed to sign. Sam much preferred the sort of history he could watch and even join in with, like the exodus. His head nodded along with his drooping eyes. It was so hard to stay awake in this stifling heat.

"Sam Parrow!" Mrs Fletcher shouted from the front of the class and Sam's head snapped up with a jerk, eyes wide open. He blushed.

"Sorry," he said. The rest of the class laughed, glad that they weren't the ones caught napping. Sighing, Mrs Fletcher returned to her desk.

"Put your books away, you might as well spend the last five minutes looking through last week's test," she said. It was far too hot to teach, she'd much rather be sat at home with an ice-cold glass of lemonade. Eventually, the bell rang and they were free to leave.

Outside the school gates, Ollie was kicking the dust created by the lack of rain.

"Sparrow!" he sneered, as Sam slouched past, too hot to bother about trying to avoid him.

Ollie grabbed Sam's jacket that was slung over his shoulder, yanking him around. A crowd began to gather, sensing the tension as the two boys faced each other.

"Fight, fight, fight!" the chant got louder as the intense heat caused everyone's tempers to rise. Sam tried to walk away but the crowd had blocked the exit. This was a fight they didn't want to miss.

Ollie lunged for Sam who managed to side-step out of the way. He swung his rucksack, catching Ollie's arm as he turned. Ollie grabbed hold of Sam and the two boys fell on the ground, rolling over as they each tried to get on top of the other. Aiming a punch at Sam, Ollie hit him just above his eye. Blood began to trickle down Sam's face onto his shirt. Unable to free himself from Ollie, Sam tried to roll himself into a ball for protection as he'd seen the pangolins do on the ark. Unfortunately, he wasn't covered in armour plating like they were and Ollie's blows rained down painfully onto his back. Being twice the size of his opponent, it was easy for Ollie to get the upper hand.

"Okay, break it up!" Mr Stevens had seen something was going on and had come out to investigate. He dragged Ollie off Sam and just missed getting hit himself. Sam uncurled himself and stood up. He wiped his face with his hands, smearing blood everywhere and making his face look far worse than it actually was. The crowd dispersed, not wanting to be seen to have encouraged the trouble.

"Oliver Jones, I expect better behaviour from my best athlete. If this happens again you'll be dropped from the team!" Mr Stevens admonished Ollie who glowered at Sam.

"Sorry sir, it won't happen again," he muttered, not meaning a word of it.

"Get yourselves off home, both of you."

Sam picked up his jacket and rucksack, watching Ollie as he sauntered off, he had no intention of heading off in the same direction.

"Are you alright?" the teacher asked.

"I'll live. Mum's going to go nuts," said Sam, looking at the state of his uniform. Mr Stevens' looked sympathetic.

"Maybe you should go back in to clean up first?" he suggested. Sam shrugged,

"It's been worse," he said, "Thanks for your help," and grinning widely Sam walked off in the opposite direction to Ollie.

The detour meant that Sam took an extra twenty minutes to get home and all he wanted when he got there was a good wash and a long cold glass of lemonade. Fortunately, his mum was in the garden so he was able to go up to his room unnoticed. Stripping out of his clothes, he sluiced his face in the sink and changed into shorts and a T-shirt. The cut above his eye had stopped bleeding but there was no way he could hide it. He could hide his uniform though so he buried it at the bottom of the laundry basket.

When Jo came in from the garden she raised her eyebrows at the cut on Sam's forehead. Sam shrugged and got out his homework. The heat was unbearable, even his mum couldn't be bothered to make a fuss and went into the kitchen to make a start on dinner.

"Will salad do?" she asked.

"Suppose. I'm not that hungry anyway."

Now Jo was concerned.

"Who is this boy in my house?" she asked.

"Ha ha, very funny! It's just too hot to eat!"

Lying in bed that night, Sam longed for the time stone to begin its hum to show that it was ready to take him on another adventure. Anywhere, thought Sam, as long as it's cooler than here! But the stone was silent and eventually, Sam drifted off into a restless sleep.

The following day, no one wanted to work, not even the biggest swots in the school. Jack had gone home early as the heat was making his foot swell uncomfortably. The cast on his broken foot felt way too tight which made him crosser than ever and Sam had spent the day making sure he was well out of his way. He had broken it the week before when he dropped a cricket ball on it and made it worse by chasing after Sam. Naturally, Jack blamed Sam, even though it was his own fault. After school, French Club was a disaster with Sam learning more French swear words from the sixth formers than he did verbs. At least there was no sign of Ollie when he made his way home. That evening, everyone was in a bad mood and Jo complained about her parents who lived nearby and who relied on her for help.

"It's stifling in their house!" she said, "They won't open any of the windows!"

Sam's dad, Andy, just turned the TV up louder. He'd had a bad day at work and was longing for the start of his annual two-week break. He was quite often able to extend it by working from home so that he could stay on at their cottage in Norfolk. However, this was looking less likely as the weeks wore on. It did not make him happy.

Bidding his parents goodnight, Sam decided to have an early night. At least there was no one to bother him in his bedroom. Settling down to read the latest book he'd got from the library, Sam glanced over at the time stone on his bedside table. As he did so, he thought he detected a faint hum. A slow grin spread from ear to ear as Sam picked up the stone and prepared for the inevitable feeling of dizziness that accompanied time travel. *I don't care where I go*, he thought, *as long as it's cool!*

CHAPTER 2

As usual, the time stone took Sam backwards in time to a small hill in Bethlehem. The sun was just beginning to peep over the horizon and a pink glow began to spread across the sky. Sounds of movement were coming from the camp as the shepherds began to wake in preparation for the start of the day. A young girl carried a large clay jar to the stream where she filled it with water before returning to the camp. Sam knew the girl, he'd visited many times already, but for now, he was content to sit and enjoy the cool breeze that came over the hill. Having delivered the water, the girl wandered over to the sheep. Sam decided it was probably time he joined her.

"Rachel!" he called as he got closer.

"Sam, it's been a while, I wasn't sure you'd be coming back!"

"How long have I been away?"

"A few weeks. You've arrived at a good time, we're moving the sheep today."

"Why, where are you taking them?"

"Only to the other side of the hill, they need fresh pasture. It will give the grass on this side chance to grow again."

"Can I help?"

"Of course, come on, you're just in time for breakfast!"

Rachel and Sam went back to the camp where they feasted on unleavened bread dipped in honey. Rachel's brothers had met Sam the first time he came to Bethlehem, on the night that Jesus was born in the stable. That was a night none of them would forget in a hurry. Of course, they didn't know that Sam had come from the future, which was a secret shared only by the two young friends.

With breakfast finished the camp was quickly packed away and the fire was put out and made safe. Eli opened the gate to the pen where the sheep had spent the night and softly called each one by name. As he moved away the sheep followed, spreading out over the grass as they walked. Rachel, Sam and Jacob walked behind, urging the stragglers to keep up. Sam was amazed at how obedient they all were.

"The sheep know their master's voice," said Rachel, "They will follow him anywhere!"

It took most of the day to move the flock to the other side of the hill as the sheep were not in any hurry and the grass was just too delicious to leave untouched. Eventually, however, the shepherds were able to set up their new camp and the sheep were settled in their pen for the night. Sam had enjoyed his day with the sheep, he had especially enjoyed the cool breeze, so unlike the weather they were having at home. After a meal of lentil stew, the two friends lay back on the grass and gazed at the stars. They had settled a little way from Eli and Jacob as they didn't want their conversation overheard and they certainly didn't want them witnessing any time stone activity!

"What happened to you?" asked Rachel, looking at the scar on Sam's forehead.

"Oh, there's a boy at school who doesn't like me," Sam replied, "His friend had an accident and now he's taking it out on me. It wasn't my fault but I guess he just likes hitting people, me especially."

"I don't understand why boys fight."

"Girls do too!"

"Not here, not usually anyway. Although I suppose some can be quite nasty with the things they say."

"I suppose they just want people to think they're better than everyone else, or at least better than the one they're fighting."

"Mmm, maybe," Rachel sat up, suddenly wide awake, "Is the time stone humming?"

Sam took it out of the pouch on his belt and grinned.

"Hold on," he said and with a flash of light the scenery changed and they found themselves standing at the top of a hill watching a very strange sight.

"What's going on?" asked Sam.

Rachel frowned, "I'm not sure," she said.

A crowd of people surrounded the hill lower down while hundreds of men danced around an altar at the top. They were chanting and wailing and beating themselves with sticks. Up above, the sun was high in the sky with not a cloud in sight, reminding Sam of the weather at home. He sighed, he had hoped he'd left it behind, he was already feeling too hot.

"Shout louder! Where is your god, is he busy? Or perhaps he is asleep and you need to awaken him!" An elderly man with grey hair and a long beard taunted the group from the sidelines. Rachel gave a start.

"Elijah!" she said, "We must be at the top of Mount Carmel." Sam looked at her questioningly so Rachel explained that during the time of the many kings that came after David, there had been a drought with no rain for three years. All the food was gone and there was no grass for the flocks.

"So what's this, a rain dance?"

"No, it's a test. Elijah challenged them to offer a sacrifice to Baal, he's the god they worship. When King Ahab married Jezebel she enticed him further away from Yahweh until all worship of Yahweh was outlawed. Elijah believes he's the last remaining prophet of the one true God."

Rachel paused as the priests of Baal danced themselves into a loud frenzy. They were becoming extremely over-excited and wild.

"Anyway," she continued, "Elijah challenged them to pray for rain but they weren't allowed to light the fire for their sacrifice, they have to get their god, Baal, to do it."

"How will that prove anything?"

"Elijah knew it wouldn't happen because Baal has no power, it's just a statue that they made themselves. Only Yahweh has the power to send fire and rain. You'll see, they'll be stopping soon and then it's Elijah's turn."

But it was evening before the priests of Baal stopped their crazy dance, by which time they were all thoroughly exhausted. Then Elijah called to the crowd.

"Come here to me." As the people moved forward up to the top of the hill, Elijah repaired the altar of the Lord which was lying in ruins after being unused for so long. Then he dug a small trench all around it and arranged the wood on top. He cut the bull that had been provided into pieces and placed them on top of the wood. Then he turned and spoke once more to the crowd.

"Fill four large jars with water and pour it onto the offering and the wood."

When they had done as Elijah asked, he told them to do it again and then again for a third time. Throughout the night the people collected water from the small river at the bottom of the hill and carried it back up to the top. The river had once been full and fast-flowing, now after three years of drought, it was reduced to a small trickle. By the time they had finished, the bull and the wood were soaked through and water dripped down filling the trench. Sam looked at Rachel, disbelief written all over his face.

"No way is that going to burn!" he said.

Rachel grinned, "Oh yeah? Just you watch."

Elijah stepped forward and prayed: "O Lord, God of Abraham, Isaac and Israel, let it be known today that you are God in Israel and that I am your servant and have done all these things at your command. Answer me, O Lord, answer me, so these people will know that you, O Lord, are God and that you are turning their hearts back again."

As soon as Elijah finished praying fire fell from heaven and burnt up the sacrifice, the wood, the stones and the soil. All the water in the trench evaporated and the people fell down in awe, declaring that the Lord was God.

Sam looked at the scene before him in amazement.

"Wow," he gasped, "That was awesome!"

CHAPTER 3

They were still standing near the top of Mount Carmel but the stone had moved them slightly forward in time. Underneath the clear blue sky, everywhere was silent except for flies buzzing around the sacrifice that was still waiting to be burnt up on top of the Baal priests' altar. The crowd had dispersed, only Elijah was left, kneeling in front of the ashes from Yahweh's fire.

"What's he doing?" whispered Sam.

"Praying for rain," Rachel whispered back.

The two children shuffled closer, careful not to make any noise that would alert Elijah to their presence. They saw the prophet speak to a man who ran off towards the edge of the cliff. When he returned, the children heard him tell Elijah there was nothing there. Rachel whispered to Sam that Elijah was sending his servant to look out to sea for the rain. In the end, Elijah sent him back seven times before the servant told him he could see a small cloud, no bigger than his hand. Straightaway, Elijah stood up and instructed his servant to go down the hill to where King Ahab was waiting with his entourage.

"Tell him to go home before the rain stops him," he said. As he was speaking, the small cloud grew bigger and was joined by more clouds which gathered as the wind grew stronger. The temperature had dropped considerably and Sam shivered. They watched Elijah tuck his cloak into his belt and run down the hill. In the distance, the children could see the king's chariot racing towards the town. Heavy rain began to fall from the black clouds overhead.

"He's overtaken the chariot, look! How on earth did he do that?" Sam spluttered, hardly able to believe his eyes.

"Yahweh is helping him to run fast. I wouldn't mind some of that help too, this rain is freezing!"

As if in answer to Rachel's plea, the time stone hummed, glowed and whisked them away.

"Phew! That's better," declared Sam, shaking raindrops out of his hair. They appeared to be inside a cave so at least they were dry. A glimmer of light came from the entrance and they could see a man was standing next to the wall.

"Isn't that Elijah?" asked Sam.

"Yes, I think so. This must be the cave where Yahweh spoke to him."

"So how close in time are we to what just happened?"

"Not long after. Jezebel threatened to kill him so he got scared and ran away. She was the worst queen ever, none of Yahweh's people were safe from her. Elijah was feeling alone and abandoned, he didn't know that there were a lot of other prophets who were safe in hiding. He thought he was the only one left."

"That can't have been much fun," said Sam making the understatement of the year.

"No," agreed Rachel.

Suddenly, a huge wind tore around the mountain, hurling up rocks and smashing them on the ground. Sam and Rachel cowered in the back of the cave as the wind howled and roared but Elijah remained steadfast near the entrance. He seemed to be looking for something but unable to find whatever it was he shook his head and sighed.

After a while the wind died down but before they had time to enjoy the peace that followed they heard a loud rumble and a crack that sounded like a pistol shot at the start of a race.

The floor of the cave moved up and down making Sam think of riding the waves on his surfboard but the movement got bigger until it was a hundred times worse. The children fell onto the floor of the cave and lay clinging to each other, terrified of what was happening. The ground continued to roll like the waves of the sea and a gaping hole appeared near the back of the cave. They tried to wedge themselves behind a rock but the rock moved and they rolled with it towards the new opening. The rock teetered on the edge until another wave sent it rolling down to who knew where. Sam managed to brace himself against the back wall while Rachel grabbed hold of another rock that was jutting out above them. Elijah somehow managed to stay upright near the entrance, holding on to the wall of the cave for support. Eventually, the ground stilled, and the children were once more able to let go of the rock, although they still clung tightly to each other. For some reason, they both felt it helped to have someone else to hold on to. Rachel gulped back a sob and wiped away her tears, she had been so sure they were going to follow the rock through the hole! Sam gripped her hand and shuddered, he'd been scared too.

The children's attention was drawn back to the entrance where they could see an orange glow bright enough to light up the inside of the cave. The sound of crackling and a faint smell of smoke told them that the mountain was on fire. Sam began to shake, he knew the stone wouldn't have brought them into danger but this was getting to be beyond a joke. Why didn't Elijah move? He was still standing there, leaning on the wall, seemingly oblivious to everything that was going on! The cave began to feel uncomfortably warm and smoke started to drift into where they were hiding, causing them to cough. Even though Rachel knew the story and knew that Elijah (and hopefully themselves) would not be harmed it wasn't fun being in the middle of it! After what seemed like an eternity, the fire died down leaving nothing but the smell of bonfires on the breeze. Rachel and Sam both breathed a sigh of relief.

A faint whisper called from outside and when he heard it, Elijah moved to the mouth of the cave and pulled his cloak over his face.

"What are you doing here, Elijah?" said the Lord, gently.

Elijah replied, "I have been very zealous for the Lord God Almighty. The Israelites have rejected your covenant, broken down your altars, and put your prophets to death with the sword. I am the only one left, and now they are trying to kill me too."

God told Elijah to return to where he had come from so that he could anoint new kings and a new prophet to take over from himself. All those who had abandoned God and worshipped Baal would be put to death. God also told Elijah that he was not alone as there were seven thousand prophets still alive who worshipped the one true God. When God had finished speaking, Elijah gathered his cloak around him, left the cave and went back to where he had come from.

In the silence that filled the cave after all the

things that had happened, Sam sat very still, listening to the whisper of a gentle breeze.

"Remember, you are not alone."

Sam looked, at Rachel, his eyes as wide as saucers, "Did you hear that?" he gasped.

Rachel nodded, her eyes as wide as Sam's, "Do you think Yahweh knows about us?"

Sam gulped, thinking of the first time Kate had travelled with him to see Jesus. It wasn't until they had got home again that she had admitted he had spoken to her.

"Yeah," said Sam shakily, "I think he does!"

CHAPTER 4

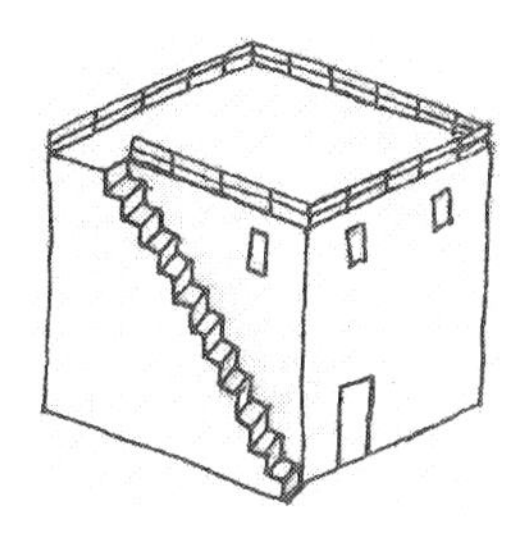

Sounds of snoring came from the shepherds' camp as Rachel and Sam shook their heads to recover their balance. They had once more travelled forwards through time to Rachel's home in Bethlehem. The stars were still twinkling in the sky and the sheep were snuffling gently in their pen. The two friends sat quietly on the hillside thinking of all the things they had seen and heard.

"Yahweh can be very scary sometimes," sighed Sam. Rachel nodded thoughtfully.

"Yes, but he can also be very gentle," she said, "I suppose he must have always known about us because he knows everything."

"Do you think he's the one that brought me here?" asked Sam, "Maybe finding the time stone wasn't an accident, maybe Yahweh put it there for me to find."

"I don't know but I'm glad you came. I know I

was scared at first but it's been such fun!"

"Even the earthquake?"

"Well, maybe not that, although it was certainly exciting!" The two children laughed, relieved that they were safely back on a hillside that was neither moving nor burning up.

Rachel yawned, "I think I'm going to move closer to the fire and sleep, it's been a long day!"

"Good idea," agreed Sam, but somewhere in between where they were and where they were going, the time stone hummed and took Sam home. The heat of the day hit him as soon as he got back, the night-time cool of Bethlehem becoming nothing more than a memory as Sam settled down to sleep.

Back in first-century Bethlehem, Rachel turned round to speak to Sam. When she saw that he was no longer there she felt quite sad and lonely, she missed her new friend when he went home. Settling down beside the fire Rachel was drifting off to sleep when she thought she heard a gentle whisper on the breeze.

"Remember my child, you are never alone."

At school, Sam steered clear of Ollie who glared angrily whenever Sam happened to glance in his direction. Jack had stayed at home so that he could keep his injured foot raised up on the sofa. Consequently, life was hot, sticky but generally trouble-free.

The inter-house cricket tournament was underway so Sam joined Kate and Alex under the shade of the sports pavilion veranda. Out on the pitch, Ollie had just gone up to bat. The three friends were debating the merits of the bowler when a faint hum sounded in Sam's pocket. He frowned, now really wasn't a good time. Kate raised her eyebrows and nodded towards Alex. Sam shrugged, were they supposed to take Alex too?

"What's that noise?" asked Alex, staring at Sam and Kate who both seemed to be acting weirdly, "What's going on?"

Sam sighed and held on to his arm, "Just don't scream!" he said, thinking of the first time Kate had accompanied him. Quickly checking that no one else was watching, Sam took out the time stone and with Kate holding on to Alex's other arm they were transported back in time to Rachel's garden.

It was the start of the day and the cool of the early morning was a welcome relief to the heat of twenty-first-century England. Rachel, now much older, was milking Hepzibah the goat, while her son, Matthew, was feeding the hens and collecting eggs. In between Sam and Kate, Alex's face was the colour of the milk in Rachel's bucket.

"Take a deep breath and stay calm," Kate spoke firmly to Alex in an attempt to stop him from freaking out, "And welcome to first-century Bethlehem!"

Alex looked as though he was about to run away, "F-first-century B-Bethlehem?" he squeaked. Kate nodded and grinned widely.

Sam walked over to Rachel, "Shalom!" he called.

"Sam, it's good to see you, it's been such a long time since yesterday!" They both laughed and Rachel sat up, stretching her back as she did so. Seeing Kate holding up Alex she smiled and said, "Oh a new friend, welcome! Come, Kate, every young woman should know how to milk a goat, let me teach you!"

Kate grinned and squatted next to Rachel while Sam led Alex over to Matthew and the hens.

"This is Rachel's son, Matthew, Matthew, meet Alex. Have you collected many eggs?" he asked.

"Not yet, why don't you look?" Matthew held out the basket to Alex while Sam went over to the nesting box. Sam put his hand in and pulled out a small brown egg, closely followed by another, slightly larger one.

"Just two I think," he said, placing them in the basket that Alex was holding.

"Two is better than none, you're just in time for breakfast!"

Inside the house, Matthew put the basket of eggs on a shelf in the cool storeroom at the back. He brought out a bowl of yoghurt and placed it on the table with a pot of honey and a bowl of dried figs. Sam washed his hands then put out spoons and bowls. Alex stood near the door watching everything that was going on. He still hadn't spoken, not feeling able to trust himself to say anything anywhere near intelligible. Both Sam and Kate looked to be very much at home, this was apparently not their first time here. He just couldn't decide if this was real or whether Ollie had hit a six and the ball had bounced off his head. At least he wasn't feeling sick and dizzy anymore.

Outside, they could hear Kate squealing as she

attempted to get milk from Hepzibah. Rachel laughed and suggested she try again another time.

"Go wash your hands while I finish, I will join you in a little while."

Kate did as she was asked then sat at the table with the three boys.

"So who won?" grinned Sam.

"Hepzibah," groaned Kate, "It's just as well you aren't relying on me for your morning milk!"

"You will learn," said Rachel from the doorway, "You just need to practise!"

Over breakfast, all four of them took turns to try to explain to Alex about the time stone and the many adventures they had all had.

"No wonder you two are so friendly!" said Alex when they had finally finished.

Sam nodded, "Now you know why it was all so awkward! You would never have believed us if we'd told you." Alex agreed that it would have been unlikely but he did think it explained a lot about why Sam seemed to be more confident.

"Why don't you show Alex the town?" suggested Rachel. "I need to bake bread and prepare the vegetables for dinner."

The three boys plus Kate headed off towards the

town square. Alex kept pulling at his tunic, not used to wearing a 'dress.'

"Leave it alone, everyone else is dressed the same," said Kate staring at him, "I've just realised, you're not wearing glasses! Can you see?"

Alex stood still and stared back at Kate. He put his hand up to his face and opened his eyes wide.

"Wow," he said, "I hadn't noticed, I can see perfectly!"

Matthew looked puzzled, "What are glasses?" he asked.

"They're things I wear over my eyes. When I'm at home my eyes don't work properly and they help me to see clearly."

"Are you blind then?"

"No, but everything is out of focus, blurred." While the others were exclaiming over Alex's perfect eyesight, Sam noticed that the time stone had started to hum.

"Quick everyone, hold on! We're going travelling!"

CHAPTER 5

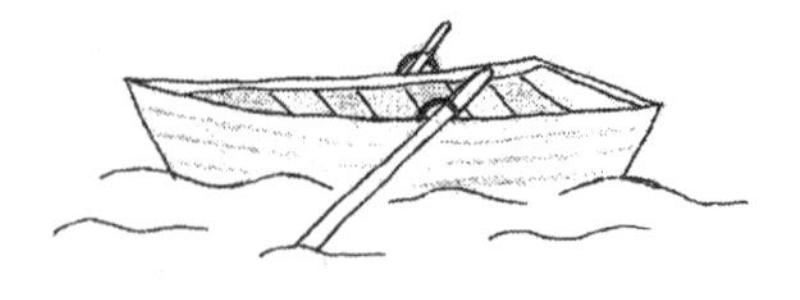

Just like the time when he was on the ark, the sick feeling that Sam always felt when travelling through time was worse. The boat they had landed on bobbed gently up and down and he gripped the sides while taking some deep breaths. Alex looked almost as terrified as he had the first time when they had arrived in Rachel's garden. Kate looked as though she was about to throw up. Only Matthew seemed to be alright so he grasped the oars on either side of the small fishing boat and looked around to see in which direction he should row. Quite a few small boats were setting off from the shore and heading across the large lake to the other side so Matthew did the same. Eventually, the others began to feel better and were able to watch what was happening around them.

"So do you think we're on the Sea of Galilee?" asked Sam, "It makes a change from being on the shore!"

"I don't know of anywhere else it could be," replied Matthew, "I wonder where everyone is going."

"Wherever it is I suppose Jesus is somewhere in the middle of it," said Kate, "Do you want some help?"

"I'm alright for now, maybe we could all take turns though, it is hard work!"

The others nodded and agreed to swap when Matthew got tired.

Although it had been morning when they left Bethlehem, here on the lake the sun had almost set and the first stars were twinkling in the sky. Fortunately, the other boats were keeping their distance from each other so that they didn't crash in the dark. The children could see lamps being lit across the lake on those boats that were equipped for fishing at night.

"There's a tarpaulin at the back, maybe there's a lamp underneath," said Sam as he lifted it up to have a look. He pulled aside a coil of rope and a tangled net but couldn't see a lamp.

"Never mind, we'll just have to make a noise so that they hear us instead!" said Kate, standing up to change places with Matthew.

"Careful, you're rocking the boat," Alex grabbed an oar to stop it from falling overboard.

"Ooops, sorry," Kate sat down and grasped the oars, "Phew, it's harder than it looks!" Kate was pulling hard on the oars but the boat didn't seem to move very far.

"Maybe we should have an oar each," Alex squeezed onto the seat beside Kate and took one of the oars from her.

Sam frowned, "You need to row the same or we'll go round in circles." Alex and Kate adjusted their pull so that they were more evenly matched.

"That's why it's better for just one person to row at a time," said Matthew.

"Yeah but it's too hard!" puffed Kate, pulling on the oar to keep in time with Alex.

"Actually I think it's getting harder," said Alex as he struggled to keep a steady pace. Sam leant over the side to look at the sea.

"The waves are getting bigger," he said. Just then a gust of wind blew across the lake, making him shiver. A dark cloud passed over the moon and fewer stars twinkled in the sky. Concerned voices could be heard coming from the other boats as the wind blew stronger and the water became very choppy, making the boat rock alarmingly.

"Where's the lifeboat when you need it?" muttered Kate.

"I think I'd settle for a miracle," groaned Sam, shaking water out of his eyes as a wave splashed over the boat and emptied itself all over him, "That was freezing!"

The boat rose up and down with the swell of the waves which appeared to be getting bigger by the minute. A huge gust of wind slammed into the side of the boat, almost capsizing them. Alex and Kate stopped rowing as they didn't seem to be making any headway and pulled the oars inside to prevent them from being swept away. They could hear cries of anguish from other boats as most of the lamps had been put out by the wind or the waves. It was now very dark and very cold. Another huge wave swept them headlong towards a large boat filled with grown men wrestling with the sail. They managed to get it down just as a wave threw itself overboard directly onto the mast. Water filled the boat and poured out over the sides.

Soaked through and frozen, Matthew, Sam, Alex and Kate clung to the sides of their tiny craft, terrified of being swept into the sea. With his stomach doing somersaults, Sam thought it was like being on a very wet roller coaster. Except everyone knew that would stop, this ride was way scarier with no sign of ending. As the waves got stronger he willed the little boat to stay upright. A large wave drove them forward towards the bigger boat. Just when they thought they would crash, a gust of wind spun them around and they passed behind it, missing it by an oar's length.

"Yahweh, help us!" whispered Sam, as he held on for dear life, shivering uncontrollably from the freezing sea. Nearby, they could hear the shouts and cries from the boat they had almost crashed into.

"Teacher, don't you care if we drown?"

The moon had appeared from behind a cloud and in its pale light, they saw one of the men go to the back of the boat where he bent over and shook whoever was there, hidden by the side. The man he had called teacher stood up.

"Jesus!" gasped Matthew.

Jesus looked out over the sea and spoke to the storm, "Quiet! Be still!" Immediately, the wind died down and the waves lessened until the sea was completely calm. In the silence that followed, the children could hear everything that Jesus said to his disciples who were with him on the boat.

"Why are you so afraid? Do you still have no faith?"

The disciples were terrified. "Who is this?" they asked each other, "Even the wind and the waves obey him!"

Matthew, Sam, Alex and Kate breathed a sigh of relief as their tiny boat drifted away from the others. They were all shaking with cold and rubbed their hands together to try to warm them up.

"That was as bad as the earthquake!" said Sam.

"Earthquake?" asked Alex, "Does this sort of thing happen often?"

"Not usually, although for me, it was just last night, it depends where we get taken back to. The earthquake happened when I was with Rachel when she was a girl. We went back to see Elijah when Yahweh spoke to him in the cave."

"Wow, so what happens now?"

Matthew, Sam and Kate all looked at each other and shrugged.

"Don't know," said Kate.

"Either we go home or we get taken somewhere else," Matthew looked at Sam, "You haven't lost the stone overboard have you?"

They all looked a little panicked until Sam brought the stone out of his pouch. Their relief at seeing it and then hearing it hum was enormous. The stone's blue light lit up the sea and before they could shake the water from their hair it had whisked them away.

CHAPTER 6

At least they were warmer. The sun was high in the sky and beating down on them as they stood on a hillside overlooking a wide valley. Their wet clothes steamed and dried in the heat. Sam looked up and guessed that it was midday as the sun was directly overhead. Through the middle of the valley, a long road ran from one end to the other. In the distance, they could see clouds of dust rising up and coming closer. As the dust clouds got nearer, they heard shouting and the sound of many running feet. While they watched, the dust clouds revealed a huge army racing through the valley with another army chasing after them in hot pursuit. The road was so long that it took some time before they were directly in front of where the four friends were standing.

"Who are they?" asked Sam.

"No idea but there's a lot of them!" answered

Matthew.

"Look at that cloud, it's acting really weird!" exclaimed Kate.

A large cloud hovered over the first army and huge hailstones rained down on them. It seemed to be following them, leaving their pursuers completely unscathed.

"Anyone would think it was attacking them," Alex shook his head, puzzled as to why the cloud only hovered over the army that was being chased, "Those soldiers have fallen down, look!" He pointed along the road to where many soldiers in the first army had been struck down by the hailstones.

"They're not moving," frowned Kate, "Why don't they get up?"

The children watched as soldiers at the back ran over those who had fallen in front of them in their haste to escape, but it was no use, the cloud sent hailstones that struck them too. Many died before their pursuers got close enough to attack. Amazingly, no matter how close the second army got to the first, the hailstones didn't touch them.

It was a long way from one end of the valley to the other and the pursuing army chased their enemy the whole way along until they had defeated them. A great cheer arose as the victors turned around and returned the way they had come. Sam wiped his face and looked up at the sun, it was still as hot as when they had arrived and they'd been there for hours.

"Er, Matthew, why hasn't the sun moved?" he asked. Sam was right, the sun was still in exactly the same place as when they had first arrived. Matthew looked up at the sky and grinned.

"I know when we are!" he said, "It's the battle for Gibeon when Joshua commanded the sun to stand still!"

"And it did? You're kidding!" Sam looked at him in total disbelief, "That's impossible!"

"The Israelites needed more time to defeat the Amorites so Joshua asked Yahweh to hold the sun and moon still until they were victorious. They needed the daylight you see, they wouldn't have been able to pursue them in the dark. Yahweh sent the hail too, that's why it only affected the first army, he kept the Israelites safe."

"I've read about it," said Alex, "But it's a whole new experience to be a part of it!"

Kate laughed, "Isn't Yahweh amazing!" she said and she twirled around with her arms outstretched. The boys joined in, thrilled to have witnessed the immense power of God who fought for those he loved. Eventually, they collapsed onto the ground, out of breath and thirsty.

"Is there a stream nearby?" asked Kate, "I could do with a drink."

"I don't know but it may be time to go home," said Sam, holding up the time stone which had started to hum.

"It's just as well," said Alex, looking up at the sky, "The sun's going down!"

The four children arrived back in Bethlehem, under the fig tree in Rachel's garden.

"Oh, you didn't get to see the town," exclaimed Matthew to Alex.

"That's okay, I've had enough excitement for one day!"

Rachel came out into the garden, "Aren't you going?" she asked, "I thought you would have been halfway there by now!"

The four friends burst out laughing and led Rachel back into the house.

"We were," said Matthew, "But we went to Galilee instead!"

"Yes, and then we spent a whole day watching

Joshua defeat the Amorites!" Sam shook his head, still amazed at how time had stood still just because Joshua had asked it to.

Rachel smiled and put water and fruit on the table.

"Help yourselves, I think you have a story to tell me!"

Refreshed with beakers of water and warm date cakes fresh out of the oven, the children took turns to tell Rachel about their adventure.

"It was amazing!" grinned Alex, who had finally relaxed enough to share in the tale, "I'm so glad you brought me!"

Sam and Kate looked at each other and grinned, "I don't think we had a choice," said Sam.

"I suppose you'll be going home now," Matthew looked at Sam who answered with a shrug.

"We will be back though, won't we?" asked Alex who had decided that first-century Israel wasn't as bad as he had first thought. After all, he'd even got used to wearing a 'dress'!

They all laughed at how Alex had changed from when he had first arrived, so scared that he couldn't speak. He didn't mind, he was just glad to have been a part of all the things that had happened, even if they had almost got shipwrecked!

"Come on, you can introduce me to Hepzibah," Alex stood up, closely followed by Kate and Sam. Matthew got up to join them when Rachel asked him to help with the chores.

"You need to take food for your Abba," she said. Matthew began to fill the basket with bread and cheese while his three friends went outside. They were just about to greet the goat when with a hum and a flash they found themselves back at the sports pavilion watching Ollie hit a six.

"He is really good isn't he?" said Alex, taking his glasses off to give them a clean. He'd enjoyed not having to wear them for a time, especially while they were in the boat. That would have been a real nuisance if they'd got wet.

"Yeah, I just don't understand why he has such a problem with me!" moaned Sam.

"It's 'cos you're so nice," Kate smiled and nudged her friend who pulled a face.

"Yeah right!" he said and blushed the colour of Kate's hair.

CHAPTER 7

Ollie strutted through the school gates, swinging his rucksack and grinning at the small group of girls standing at the bottom of the steps. His superb performance the day before at the inter-house cricket tournament had helped his team secure the junior house trophy. He had also won player of the match which had finally secured his father's approval. How long that would last for though, Ollie could only guess, hopefully for the next two days at least. It would be good to have a whole weekend without complaints and snide remarks. Maybe his dad would let him off training on Saturday so he could visit Jack. Ollie sighed, no, probably not.

His dad had been a sergeant in the army and destined for glory, representing his regiment in the pentathlon. He'd had high hopes of being selected for the Olympics until a bad fall from his horse ended his sporting career. Sergeant Jones had left the army and now took his frustrations out on his son. The truth was that Ollie bullied Sam because Sergeant Jones bullied him.

Sam shut his locker just as Ollie pushed past. There was plenty of room for him to get round Sam but where was the fun in that?

"Well if it isn't the little sparrow! Won any fights lately? Or are you too busy playing house with the redhead?"

Sam took a deep breath and silently asked Yahweh for help. Turning round he looked up at his tormentor and forced himself to smile.

"You mean Kate? She's too cool to play house. Great fun though. We watched you yesterday, you played really well."

Ollie frowned, taken aback by Sam's response. He didn't expect him to be so.... normal.

"Yeah, well I'm the best, I always play well, unlike some!" he sneered. Sam shrugged.

"We can't all be like you. I'm just better at other stuff."

"Like what?"

"Dunno, I'm still trying to find out!" Sam laughed and walked away, his heart pounding after standing up to his rival.

Ollie watched him go and shook his head, disbelief written all over his face. Was that really Sam Parrow, the little squirt who ran away every time he and Jack got anywhere near? It must be the heat, he thought, it was making everyone act out of character. He wished it would rain so everything could go back to how it was!

Later, at youth group, Sam told the others about his encounter that morning with Ollie.

"Hey, well done!" declared Jamie.

"Do you think he'll leave you alone now?" asked Ben.

"I doubt it, he'll probably be even worse. I'm just glad that Jack isn't around to join in."

"Well at least you stood up to him," said Kate, "Maybe he'll think twice before he does anything else."

They all agreed that Sam had risen to the occasion and proved himself worthy of honour. That didn't stop them from going all out to beat him at air hockey though.

"Yes!" shouted Ben as he scored the winning goal, "I am the champion!"

Sam laughed as he cheerfully surrendered his title.

"I guess I'm still trying to find what it is I'm best at," he said. Chris had been watching the game and he grinned at Sam.

"You are best at being you," he said, "God made you exactly as you are for a reason. No one else is like you, you are unique."

"Doesn't it say that somewhere in the bible?" asked Kate. Chris nodded.

"There are several verses that talk about who we are. David writes that God knew us even before we were born and it was God who put us together in our own special way. Jeremiah talks about God having plans for each of us and in the New Testament, Paul writes about the different gifts that God has given us to help us succeed in those plans."

"But what if we never find out what his plans are?" asked Sam.

"Some people don't but that's usually because they're not looking," answered Chris, "A lot of people prefer to go their own way and never think to ask God if what they are doing is right for them."

"A lot of people don't even believe in God!" declared Alex, whose recent experience of time travel meant that he was now totally amazed that anyone could ever think that.

"No," agreed Chris, "but even some of those that do believe don't ask him for direction in the choices they make. There are some who think that God is there to help when they're in trouble or in need of something but they still want to live their life their way, not his."

Sam thought about what Chris had said but still couldn't quite agree. Ollie obviously didn't believe in God, the things he said and did to Sam were proof of that. Yet he was successful in everything, he was smart, athletic and had the sort of looks that caused the girls to fall over themselves to be with him. Not that Sam wanted any of that but he would like to be good at something!

"So what about all the people who don't believe but who still do well? The rich and famous ones and people who get awards and stuff," he asked.

Chris laughed, "You know Sam, one of the things you're very good at is asking great questions!" Sam grinned, it certainly helped that Chris was so easy to talk to.

"The usual answer is to ask if those people are truly satisfied with their achievements," Chris continued, "Of course, they are the only ones who can answer that and sometimes it does seem that there are people who do have everything going for them. But I think you'll find that most people have something hidden away that they don't want others to know about. They may be afraid of the future, of losing everything they've worked so hard to achieve or just plain lonely. Being rich and famous brings problems of its own."

Jamie nodded, "The village where my grandparents live is the happiest I know but the people there have a lot less than we do."

"Because they are satisfied with what they do have," smiled Chris.

"But shouldn't we want to improve ourselves? I mean it's not wrong to have more than someone else is it?" Ben frowned, he was fed up with being told he should be grateful for the things he had when others in the world were starving.

"No of course it's not wrong and yes, God does expect us to make the best of every opportunity. The important thing is to ask God what you should do with the things he has given you. As

Jeremiah said, God has plans for us, we all have a job to do to make our world a better place. Paul takes this further by saying that we each have a part to play and that God has given us all the particular gifts and skills we need. These will help us to be the people he has created us to be, doing the things he has created us to do. The problems arise when we are selfish and only use those gifts to help ourselves."

Sam thought about Elijah who had such a hard time, even though he seemed to be doing everything God asked him to do.

"But even when we do the right thing there's no guarantee that everything will be okay," he said.

"You're right Sam, there isn't. The important thing though is that we still do the right thing!"

Chris looked curiously at Sam. He was surprised at how much he seemed to know and understand. Most kids Sam's age hadn't got any further than God being like a loveable Father Christmas. Maybe God had something really special in mind for Sam Parrow!

CHAPTER 8

Lying in bed that night, Sam tossed and turned as he tried to get to sleep. His mum had put a fan in the room to help circulate the air, it helped a bit but the room was still too hot. The conversation with Chris about doing the right thing kept going round and round in his head. He truly didn't mind that Ollie was so much better than him, Sam was quite happy with his lot in life. After all, he was a Time Traveller! He did mind about the bullying though, it wasn't fair, why did Ollie have to be so mean to him? The thoughts in his head were so loud that it was a while before Sam realised that the time stone was humming. As he reached out to grab it from his bedside table the stone immediately flashed its blue light and transported Sam back to Bethlehem.

Sam pushed open the door to the house, calling a greeting as he did so.

"Shalom Rachel, shalom Matthew, it's Sam!"

Rachel looked up from where she was sitting on

a stool sorting through a basket of wool.

"Sam, shalom! Are you alone this time?"

"Yes, I was in bed, it's night-time back home."

Rachel laughed, "I'm afraid you've just missed Matthew. He's taken the basket of food I was preparing for his Abba. You and your friends have only just left us!"

Sam shook his head, "That was yesterday!" he grinned. Time travel was incredibly confusing which was why his friends always made a point of telling Sam how long he'd been away. When he had first met Matthew, Sam had just left twelve-year-old Rachel after seeing the newborn baby, Jesus. It was a real shock to meet her again just an hour later when Matthew took him home. Not only had he seen the now grown-up Jesus, but he had also discovered that Rachel was Matthew's mum!

"Now you're here you can help me wind this wool. I need to make a new tunic for Matthew, his old one is too short!"

Sam pulled up a stool and sat opposite Rachel, watching her as she wound wool onto a flat wooden stick.

"This is called a shuttle. Here, you carry on with this one while I start another. This will be a long tunic to wear for when he is not running around after the sheep so I will need a lot of wool."

"Is this from your sheep?" asked Sam as he struggled to wind the shuttle. He was beginning to get the hang of it but he was nowhere near as fast as Rachel.

"Yes, the men shear the sheep at the start of summer then take it to the market to be sold. Some we keep to weave into clothes and blankets for ourselves. This is the end of last year's wool, they will begin the shearing again soon so Adah and I will be busy washing and spinning. When it is finished, we celebrate!"

"Does Matthew help you?"

"No, he helps with the shearing. This is women's work but I thought perhaps you wouldn't mind," Rachel smiled as Sam nodded his agreement.

"I don't. Chores aren't usually split up like that where I live. Men and women generally have a go at most things. Not always though, I guess it depends on what you're good at."

"And what are you good at Sam?"

Sam shrugged, "I don't know yet. My rabbi thinks I'm good at asking questions but most of those come from my trips here with you."

"So what question has brought you to us this

time?"

"Why do some people seem to have all the luck!"

"Luck? What is that?"

"Er, getting the best of everything without even trying, even when they don't deserve it. It's not fair!" moaned Sam.

"Ah, you mean fate, those things we experience that we have no control over. Do you not like the life Yahweh has given you Sam?"

"Yes, I do, especially since I've been coming here. And I don't mind that Ollie can do everything I can't, I just wish he wouldn't brag about it all the time."

"Oh, I remember you once came after you had been fighting. Was it with him?"

"Yes, and it was the day before yesterday, look, I still have the scar!"

"Oh my goodness but that was years ago! No wonder you get confused! Wasn't that when we went to see Elijah and were in the earthquake? I remember I was very frightened."

"So was I and then we heard Yahweh speak to us. I think that was even scarier!"

"But I have never forgotten what he said, he told us that we were not alone. You should remember that, Sam. Yahweh is with you all the time, even when things seem to be going wrong."

"Chris, my rabbi, said that Yahweh has plans for us and has given us everything we need to do the things he wants us to do. The trouble is I don't know what it is I'm supposed to do!"

"Well you are still very young, there's plenty of time to find out. Just make sure you do what is right and keep listening for his voice. Don't forget, it may only be a whisper but you will recognise it, just like the sheep recognise the voice of their shepherd."

"Yes, you said that yesterday when we moved the sheep to the other side of the hill!"

They both laughed at the difference in time for each of them. Things that had been said and done so recently for Sam had happened over thirty years ago for Rachel. Sam put down the shuttle that was now full with the wool he had wound while they were talking. A low hum sounded from the pouch that hung from his belt.

"I think we may be going somewhere," he said, taking the time stone out of his pouch. Rachel held onto Sam's arm and smiled.

"I was hoping we would be!" she said.

CHAPTER 9

Sam and Rachel were standing in the courtyard of a large house. They were dressed as they were when they met Daniel, Shadrach, Meshach and Abednego for the first time at King Nebuchadnezzar's palace in Babylon. In front of them, Daniel sat on a bench in the shade of a tree.

"I think he'll be surprised to see us again," grinned Sam.

"Yes, but he doesn't look very happy, I wonder when we've arrived?"

Daniel looked up and saw the two travellers, "Shalom," he said, "Do I know you? You look familiar."

"Shalom," greeted Rachel, moving closer, "we met you and your friends when you were students at the palace. We needed your help with the translation of some Hebrew script."

Daniel gasped and peered closely at the two

people standing in front of him.

“Rachel? You look no different to how you were then! But were there not two boys with you?”

“Yes, only Samuel has come with me this time. It has only been a few weeks for us although it seems as though a few years have passed for you.”

“Indeed,” replied Daniel, “Much has happened since that time. I have wondered about you and the story you told. I confess that I didn’t entirely believe you, now perhaps I think I must!”

Rachel nodded, “It is not an easy story to believe!”

“Forgive me, my lady, please sit with me.” Daniel moved along the bench to make room for Rachel and Sam.

“Thank you. We are not sure when we have arrived but you seem troubled. Is there anything we can help you with?”

Daniel sighed, “I’m afraid that Yahweh has spoken great judgement on Nebuchadnezzar. He dreamt of a magnificent tree that bore much fruit and gave shelter to many animals and birds. Then he saw the tree destroyed with only the root left in the ground. Nebuchadnezzar has become extremely powerful and proud but still refuses to acknowledge that everything he has is given to him by Yahweh. I'm afraid he will suffer greatly until he confesses his sin and does what is right."

"Oh Daniel, I'm so sorry that you had to deliver this message to him," said Rachel, "Nebuchadnezzar does indeed suffer for seven years but be at peace. At the end of the time, he will acknowledge the Lord and his kingdom will be returned to him."

Sam gasped, "Rachel, should you have told him that? I thought we weren't supposed to know the future!"

Daniel smiled, "Do not worry my friend, Yahweh already spoke of this in the dream. I merely wanted to spare the king his suffering but it seems that he must follow the path set before him."

Sam frowned, he was remembering what had happened at the tower of Babel.

"Yahweh really doesn't like us to ignore him does he?"

"No he doesn't," agreed Rachel, "But he does allow us the freedom to choose. Unfortunately, people don't always like the results of their choices! Yahweh has already warned Nebuchadnezzar but the King wouldn't listen, he chose to honour himself rather than the Lord."

"Yes, Yahweh reserves his hardest judgements

for those who have received the highest rewards in life." Daniel smiled, finally at peace with the message that he had been given to speak. "Yahweh's decision is made and we will not question it. Now, tell me about the exciting things you have seen!"

For the next hour, Rachel and Sam shared with Daniel some of their adventures. He especially liked their stories about the ark, laughing when Sam told him about the gorilla that treated Sam as if he was her baby!

A servant came into the courtyard to say that Daniel had a visitor. As he stood up to go inside the house, Sam raised his eyebrows at Rachel. Guessing his question, she nodded.

"Erm, I think we should say shalom," Sam said, "We will probably have left by the time you get back."

"Yes, I'm sure you are right," Daniel inclined his head towards Rachel, "Shalom, my lady, Samuel. Perhaps Yahweh will allow us to meet again."

"Oh, I do hope so. We have enjoyed speaking with you," Rachel smiled, "Shalom, Daniel, may the Lord bless you."

Daniel followed his servant into the house, leaving Rachel and Sam alone in the courtyard. The time stone hummed and in a flash, they were transported to the rooftop of Nebuchadnezzar's palace.

CHAPTER 10

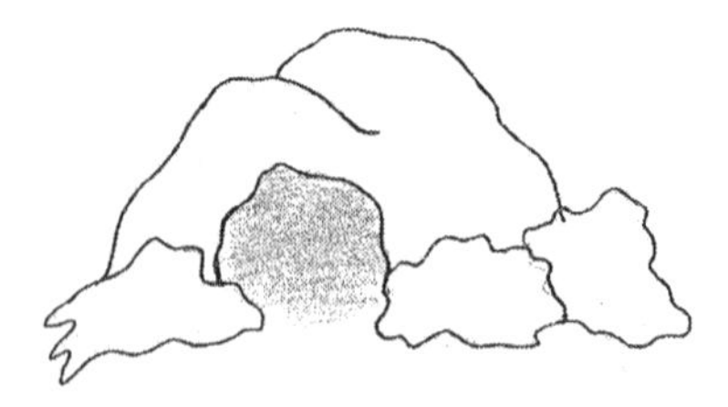

Nebuchadnezzar walked around the roof, admiring the great city spread out below him. He felt very pleased with himself and declared that he was the greatest king that ever lived. Suddenly, a loud voice spoke from heaven.

"King Nebuchadnezzar, listen! Your royal power has been taken away from you. You will be driven away to live with the wild animals and eat grass for seven years. At the end of that time, you will acknowledge that the Most High God is supreme over all man's kingdoms and gives them to whoever he chooses."

Immediately, the king ran down the stairs into the palace, closely followed by Sam and Rachel. Nebuchadnezzar tore at his robe, pulling it off and leaving it on the floor at the bottom of the stairs. He ran wildly from room to room, knocking over chairs and crashing into walls. He was making strange noises, like a frightened animal that was trapped and unable to find its way out.

Servants appeared who tried to calm the king but they only made him worse. Eventually, Daniel arrived and was able to lead the king out of the palace and out of the city gates into the fields beyond. As soon as the king reached the open fields he ran off, leaving his shoes and his outer garments behind. Sam and Rachel caught up with Daniel who was watching the king in anguish.

"It has been a full year since the dream," he said, "And not once has the king repented of his sins or acknowledged Yahweh's sovereign power."

"What will happen to him?" asked Sam.

"He will live with the animals until Yahweh restores his sanity," sighed Daniel, "There is nothing we can do except look after his kingdom until he returns." Saddened by what he had seen, Daniel went back into the city to rule over the kingdom until Yahweh gave it back to Nebuchadnezzar.

Sam looked at Rachel, horrified by what had just taken place. "That's horrendous!" he said.

"I know, but sometimes the only way for people to believe in Yahweh's power is for them to experience it for themselves." Rachel pursed her lips crossly, "It would be so much better if people were not so proud and admitted their mistakes!"

Sam pulled a face as he realised that his friend Rachel was no longer the young girl he had first met on the hillside. Now she was not only old enough to be his mother, she sometimes sounded like her too! He was just about to ask what happened next when the time stone began to hum. Sam took it out of his pouch and holding Rachel by the hand they were whisked away to a field on the side of a hill.

"So why are we here?" asked Sam, looking around for clues to where they might be.

"I don't know unless Nebuchadnezzar is around somewhere."

The two friends scanned the hillside but couldn't see anything except a few rocks and thistles in amongst the long grass.

"What's up there?" asked Sam, "Is that a cave?"

"Maybe, let's go and look. Perhaps he's taken shelter in there."

As they drew closer they could hear snuffling and an occasional low grunt. Moving quietly so as not to disturb whatever was in there, Rachel and Sam edged their way towards the back of the cave. Curled up in the corner they could see what looked like a small hairy beast that was fast asleep. The smell reminded them of the time they had spent on the ark, helping to care for all the animals.

"Is that him?" whispered Sam.

"I think so. It's hard to tell but I've never seen an animal that looks like that, not even on the ark."

Sam knelt down and gently stroked the thick hair that covered Nebuchadnezzar's body.

"At least he'll be warm with all this hair," he said.

"Yes, I suppose so. His nails need cutting though!" Rachel pointed to his hands and feet. Sam shuddered.

"Was he really so bad that Yahweh had to do this?"

"I think you know the answer to that, Sam. Remember how you felt when he ordered Daniel's friends to be thrown into the fire?"

Sam remembered how upset he had been when he and Rachel had seen King Nebuchadnezzar order his guards to throw Shadrach, Meshach and Abednego into the fiery furnace. Yahweh had saved the three friends but it was so hot that the guards had been killed just by being too close.

"Yeah, I guess so. He just seems so pathetic now though. I can't help feeling sorry for him."

"I know, I do too. I wonder how much longer he

has to stay like this?"

"Didn't Yahweh say seven years?"

"Yes, but we don't know when we have arrived. It does look as though we may be near the end of it though. I'm sure it would have taken that long for him to get into this state!"

At that moment Nebuchadnezzar woke up and scrabbled to his hands and feet. He shook himself and yawned. His breath smelt something awful! Sam wrinkled his nose.

"Pooh, he needs to clean his teeth!"

The creature that was once a king bowed his head and gently nudged Sam.

"Hey, do you want to go outside?" Nebuchadnezzar grunted and nudged him again so Sam led him out of the cave into the sunshine. Still on all fours, he began to nibble on the long grass while Sam and Rachel watched. Slowly working his way down the hillside, Nebuchadnezzar occasionally stopped to look around as he chewed.

"Why has Yahweh brought us here, Rachel?" asked Sam, sadly.

"I'm not sure, but I do think we need to be kind to Nebuchadnezzar. It is not good for him to be alone, perhaps he will allow us to be friends."

Sam thought that this was a good idea so he walked down the hill and put his arms around his hairy neck to hug him. Nebuchadnezzar stopped chewing and moaned softly.

"It's alright," said Sam, "I won't hurt you." Sam stroked Nebuchadnezzar's head and told him how much Yahweh loved him.

"But you have to change. You can't be how you used to be. Yahweh made everyone and he loves us all the same. He doesn't like it when we're hurtful and cruel to each other. You have to be good and kind and then Yahweh will give you back your kingdom."

The man who was once a great king bowed his head and tears fell from his eyes. Sam looked at Rachel in despair as Nebuchadnezzar shuddered and raising his head to the sky, bellowed loudly. It was such a mournful sound that Sam felt as though his heart would break.

"Just tell Yahweh you're sorry," he said, "I know he'll forgive you." The once-great king turned his head to look at Sam. His eyes were so sad that Sam burst into tears.

"I don't care how bad you were, you can't stay like this!" he said, wiping his nose on the back of his hand.

Lowing gently, Nebuchadnezzar nuzzled Sam and a deep groan rose from his chest that seemed to rumble with sorrow. In the silence that followed, a cool breeze ruffled the hair that covered his back. He stood up, shaking himself and stretching, rising up to stand on two legs once more. As he did so he was transformed into the man he used to be. He was still unkempt, his hair and nails still needed cutting and he definitely needed a bath but his mind was restored and it was a normal man who now stood in the field. He looked at Sam and smiled.

"Thank you," he said, "You have been very kind. You helped me to understand how wrong I have been." Sam sniffed away his tears, thrilled that the king was no longer like a creature that ate grass but was a normal man once more.

Nebuchadnezzar raised his eyes to heaven and praised Yahweh, the God of the universe. He acknowledged that Yahweh was Lord of all the world and everything in it and he could do whatever he pleased. When he had finished, Rachel gave him her shawl to wrap around himself and he went down the hillside back to Babylon. As he got closer to the city, guards on the gate saw him and called for the leaders to go out to meet him. Sam looked anxiously at Rachel.

"He'll be fine, Sam," she said, "They will accept him back and he will rule the kingdom wisely with Yahweh's help."

Sam breathed a sigh of relief and allowed the time stone to take them home.

Sam sat at the table and put his head in his hands, seeing King Nebuchadnezzar in such a sorry state had really upset him. Rachel stood behind the stool and gave Sam a hug. This was one time he didn't mind that Rachel was now more like his mum.

"I know you're upset," she said, "But remember that after he returned, Nebuchadnezzar worshipped Yahweh for the rest of his days and Yahweh rewarded him by expanding his kingdom even further."

"I just wish he hadn't needed such an awful lesson!"

"Unfortunately that's the only way some people learn. Just you make sure you're not one of them!"

Sam shook his head in horror, "I won't be!" he insisted.

Rachel went back to her basket of wool and

started to collect it up.

"Matthew should be back soon," she said, turning round to speak to Sam, only to find that the stool he had been sat on was empty. She smiled and nodded to herself, "Shalom, Sam, I'll see you again soon I hope."

Once more in his bed in the twenty-first century, Sam settled down to sleep. Exhausted from all the things that he had seen it wasn't long before his eyes closed and his gentle snores drifted round the room.

CHAPTER 11

The sun shone as brightly on Saturday as it had throughout the week and Sam arranged to meet his friends from Youth Group at the lake in the centre of the park. It was a popular place for swimming and with the weather being so hot, a great place to cool off. Alex, Ben and Jamie were already in the water so Sam quickly stripped down to his swimmers and jumped in. The four friends had a great time swimming, diving and generally splashing around.

A shout from the bank made them stop and look up to see Kate and Dayle had arrived with a ball. The girls swam over to them and they had fun throwing the ball and splashing after it. Other kids joined in and before long an energetic game of water polo started up. The game ended in a draw which resulted in a water fight with everyone finishing up on the shore, tired but happy. Sam and his friends lay on the grass to dry off in the sun.

“Anyone for ice cream?” asked Jamie. Cries of, "Yes please!" came from the others as they dug around in their belongings for cash. Orders were taken and Ben, Jamie and Dayle went off to the kiosk to fulfil their requests. Sam took the opportunity of being alone with Alex and Kate to tell of his latest adventure with Rachel and Nebuchadnezzar.

“That must have been dreadful for him,” sighed Kate.

“Yeah, how could God do that to people, even if they are bad!” agreed Alex.

“I don’t know but Rachel said that afterwards, he was one of the most humble kings ever. He worshipped God all the time and he was rewarded with more power and riches than he had before.”

“God wouldn’t do that to anyone now though, would he?” Kate looked in horror at Sam, at the thought that anything like that could happen to people they knew. Sam shrugged.

“Who knows? The thing is, Nebuchadnezzar had been warned and he had lots of time to put things right. Plus, he was a king, he had everything he could ever want! I suppose he thought he was better than everyone else and got greedy."

"Yeah, the more you have, the more you want. Me, I'd just be happy with my ice cream before it melts!" said Alex as he looked up and saw Jamie approaching with ices in each hand. Dayle and Ben followed close behind and they handed their purchases over to the three who were waiting. Contented sighs came from each of them as they sat enjoying the delight of ice cream on a hot day.

Nearby, Ollie sat watching the group. He had thought about joining the water polo until he had seen Sam swimming around in the middle of it. Their recent encounter, when Sam had calmly answered him back had made him reluctant to say or do anything in public. If ever he met him alone though, well, that would be different! Muttering angrily about all the things he'd like to do to Sam next time he got him on his own, Ollie waded into the lake and dived underwater. He was missing his friend Jack, Saturdays were no fun on his own.

Coming up to the surface, Ollie flipped onto his back and swam lazily towards the centre of the lake. He thought about the coming holidays and hoped that Jack would be able to have his cast off in time for them to do all the things they had planned. Ollie knew that it wasn't Sam's fault that Jack had broken his foot but that didn't stop him from blaming Sam for spoiling every day since.

In the middle of the lake was a small island that was surrounded by buoys strung together by rope. A sign warned people to keep away as there were nesting birds and underwater hazards. Ollie grinned and ignoring the sign he dived under the rope and swam towards the island. As he got closer he could see rocks lying just beneath the surface. He very carefully swam round them and then pulled himself up onto the bank. A duck swam out of the reeds, followed by a line of five ducklings. She quacked loudly when Ollie threw a stone in her direction, it missed but caused a large splash. Ollie laughed as the ducklings paddled closer to their mother.

Eventually getting bored, Ollie eased himself back into the water and started to swim back to shore. Just as he dived under the rope a small rowing boat went past, sending waves washing back to the island. Caught unawares, the wash pushed Ollie back onto the rocks hidden beneath the surface. Scraping his arm on the sharp surface of the rock, Ollie tried to push himself off and stand up but the rocks were too jagged and hurt his feet. He swam towards the reeds in the hope of finding softer ground, disturbing the ducks' nest as he did so. Now able to stand, Ollie inspected his arm. It was badly scraped and very sore. He swore, it would probably be stiff tomorrow and he was playing in the county under thirteen cricket team.

Ollie swam back across the lake and flung himself onto the bank, angry tears falling down his face. He knew he needed to go home so that his mum could treat his arm but he also knew that his dad would yell at him for being stupid. At least tomorrow's match would stop his dad from giving him a beating, he wouldn't want to risk him being unable to play at all. Ollie collected up his stuff and headed out of the park, there was no point in delaying it any longer.

Further along the bank, Sam watched as Ollie picked up his towel. He could see that Ollie's arm was sore and the way he was using it showed Sam that it was painful. He wondered what he had done but decided that Ollie wouldn't thank him for asking. Sam shrugged, it wasn't any of his business anyway.

CHAPTER 12

At Youth Group on Friday, Chris had invited those who were interested in learning more about Jesus to a bible study in his home. Sam decided that it was probably about time he got serious about reading the bible so he had agreed to go along. Besides, it would give him another opportunity to put his growing list of questions to Chris. The meeting was to be after the evening service on Sunday and Sam did wonder about going along to that too but decided that maybe he would save that for another week.

Chris lived on the other side of town, not far from Kate. When Sam arrived, Chris' wife opened the door, causing him to gasp in surprise.

"Miss Fielding!" he said, feeling his face flush, "I didn't know you knew Chris."

"Oh I'm Mrs Peters now, Chris and I have been married for almost a year. Come on in, your friends are already here," she grinned, "and call me Sue, we're not at school now!"

Miss Fielding had been Sam's year 5 teacher and she was one of his favourites. She knew his mum well although they taught in different schools. Sam thought that would have been too weird to go to the same school his mum taught in!

"So, how come you didn't come to the barbecue? Mum would have liked to have seen you again."

"Yes, Chris told me they came. I was away on a training course that weekend otherwise I would have been there. Maybe you could all come for tea during the summer holidays, it would be good to catch up."

Sam followed Sue into the lounge and grinned when he saw Kate, Alex and Ben already sprawled on beanbags and cushions. He recognised a few others from the group as he squeezed in beside his friends. Dayle was handing out squash and biscuits when Jamie came in and threw himself down onto a beanbag next to Sam. The room was buzzing with chatter when Chris walked in with his guitar.

"Hey, good to see you all!" he said, sitting on a

dining chair near the window, "Let's start with a few songs of praise."

The group joined in enthusiastically, singing songs they knew well. Eventually, Chris called a halt and asked God to direct their thoughts as they studied his word. Sue read a short passage from Matthew's gospel and everyone looked at Chris expectantly.

"So, why do you think Jesus tells us to love our enemies? Do you think he's asking too much?" Chris looked around the room where most of the group were nodding their heads. Those that were not, wore expressions that said, yeah, they knew they should but.....

"I suppose if we did as he asked we'd stand out from the crowd," said Jamie, "Not sure I can though."

"Well done for being honest," said Chris, "But you're right. Jesus is asking us to be different to everyone else. Loving our enemies would show people that we honour Jesus, even when it's difficult."

"It's not like we have real enemies though is it?" asked Kieran, one of the older members of the group, "I mean, we don't get persecuted like some people do in other countries."

"No we don't, but there are still people who insult us and bully us because we're not like them."

Jamie nodded, being Ghanaian he had plenty of experience of that. Chris looked at Sam and smiled in encouragement,

"What do you think, Sam?"

"You mean Ollie?" Sam asked.

Chris nodded, "From what I've heard he seems to be exactly the sort of person Jesus is talking about."

"So who's Ollie?" asked Kieran. Not everyone in the group went to Sam's school and they didn't know of his ongoing troubles. Sam considered what he should say. It would be so easy to dismiss Ollie as a troublemaker and a bully but Sam felt that God would be disappointed in him if he did. After all, he'd seen Nebuchadnezzar at his worst and still managed to feel sorry for him. Even Ollie was nowhere near as bad as he was.

"For some reason, Ollie doesn't like me and goes out of his way to show it."

His friends raised their eyebrows at this huge understatement. Ben rolled his eyes, he would say exactly what he thought of Ollie if it was him being bullied.

“So, what do we all think Sam should do?” asked Chris. Everyone shrugged their shoulders not knowing what to say.

“Be nice to him?” asked Clare who was lucky enough to have everyone always be nice to her so she didn’t really understand Sam’s problem. She just put it down to boys being boys.

“Actually, he already is,” said Alex who was keen to stand up for his friend.

Kate agreed, “Sam has been amazing, especially recently.”

“Maybe we could pray for Ollie?” suggested Jamie. Chris smiled.

“Now we’re getting somewhere,” he said, “There’s a verse in Galatians about supporting each other. Could you read it for us, Sue?”

“Carry each other’s burdens, and in this way you will fulfil the law of Christ.”

Kieran looked thoughtfully at Chris, “So what you’re saying is that Ollie’s bullying is Sam’s burden and we can help Sam by praying for Ollie?”

“Exactly,” replied Chris, “but we can pray for Sam too so that he makes the right choices. I’m sure there must be times when he feels like fighting back."

"Who wouldn't!" declared Ben, whose sense of justice meant that he may not be quite so forgiving.

Sam nodded, "Thanks, I need all the help I can get, especially when he's in a bad mood!"

The group laughed and they finished their discussion by praying for the two boys.

"And thank you God for bringing Sam to Youth Group!" added Kate.

Sam walked home that night feeling a lot happier. Nothing had changed but now he felt as though he belonged and had good friends who cared about him. A roll of thunder sounded in the distance and a streak of lightning flashed across the sky. Sam shivered, while he had been at Chris' the temperature had dropped and dark clouds gathered overhead. As he turned into his street large drops of rain began to fall. By the time he got home, Sam was soaked. He stood in the doorway and laughed. Lifting his face to the sky Sam enjoyed the refreshing rain as it cooled everything down.

"Thanks God," he laughed, "That's just what we needed!"

GLOSSARY

Abba - *Dad, daddy*

Disciples - *students*

Enticed - *tempted*

Entourage - *an accompanying group of people*

Ima - *Mum, mummy*

Intelligible - *able to be understood*

Oblivious - *unaware of something*

Pangolin - *small scaly anteater*

Pentathlon - *Olympic sport consisting of 5 events*

Persecute - *ill treatment given because of beliefs*

Prophet - *someone who speaks God's words*

Rabbi - *teacher*

Shalom - *peace, often said as a greeting*

Stadion - *Greek origin of stadium*

Steadfast - *stands firm/unwavering*

Taunted - *provoked*

BIBLE REFERENCES

If you would like to read about the events and places that Sam visited you will find them in the Christian bible. There are lots of different translations but one of the easiest to understand is the Good News Bible.

Old Testament Stories

Elijah – On Mount Carmel – *1 Kings ch 18 vs 16 - 46*

In the Cave – *1Kings ch 19 vs 7 – 18*

The day the sun stood still – *Joshua ch 10 vs 1 - 15*

Nebuchadnezzar – *Daniel ch 4*

Known by God – *Psalm 139*

God's plans – *Jeremiah ch 29 vs 11*

New Testament Stories

Jesus calms the storm – *Mark ch 4 vs 35 - 41*

God's gifts – *Romans ch 12 vs 6 - 8*

Loving our enemies – *Matthew ch 5 vs 43 – 48*

Be kind – *Ephesians ch 4 vs 32*

Helping each other – *Galatians ch 6 vs 2*

The modern pentathlon is an Olympic sport which has five separate events all held on one day. These are fencing, 200 m freestyle swimming, show jumping and the laser run. The laser run consists of shooting a pistol at five targets which must be hit before the competitor runs an 800 m lap. They have to do this four times. The events were chosen to represent the skills needed by a cavalry officer fighting behind enemy lines.

It is called the modern pentathlon because the sport in ancient times reflected the skills needed by Greek soldiers at that time. These were wrestling, long jump, javelin and discuss throwing and the stadion foot race. This race was a 200 yard (180 m) sprint which was considered to be the highlight of the Olympics, rather like our modern day 100 m sprint. Only men took part, women were not allowed to compete even in the modern pentathlon until the year 2000, although they have competed in the World Championship since 1981.

Gold medallists in the 2020 Olympics were Joe Choong and Kate French, both from Great Britain.

Sam is fortunate to live in a country that allows Christians to attend church and worship God in whatever way they choose. He knows that he is safe and will not come to any harm by doing so. Unfortunately, some countries have very strict laws that prevent people from worshipping God in public. To do so could mean imprisonment, torture and even death.

We call these people that are not allowed to worship, "persecuted Christians."

Jesus talks about them in Matthew's gospel, chapter 5 verses 10-12.

"....Blessed are you when people insult you, persecute you and falsely say all kinds of evil against you because of me. Rejoice and be glad, because great is your reward in heaven...."

Jesus knew that there would be many problems

for believers and he wanted to encourage them to be steadfast in their faith. During their time of persecution, believers in the 1st century had a special sign that they used to let others know where it was safe to meet. It looked like a fish and was made up of the letters I ch th u s

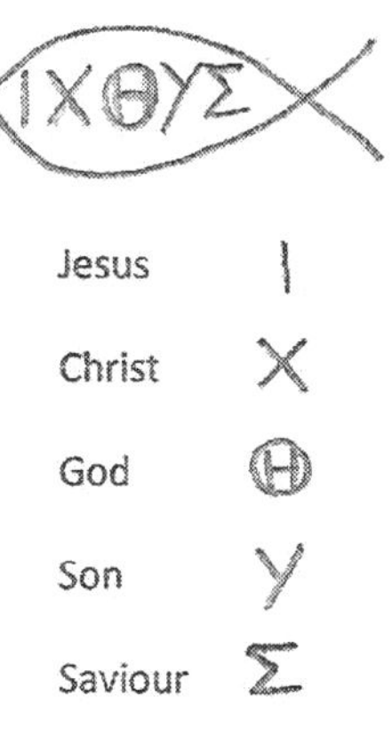

How would you feel if you couldn't share your faith with your best friend in case they told the police and got you arrested? (Yes, some countries put kids in prison too!)

Or what if you knew your parents were believers even though you weren't? Would you tell on them?

How good are you at keeping secrets? In some countries your life may depend on it!

"Open Doors" is an organisation that helps and supports persecuted Christians around the world. If you want to find out more they have an excellent children's section with ideas for helping and fun stuff to do.

As always, do check with your responsible adult before going on the internet.

www.opendoorsuk.org/resources/children-at-home

ACKNOWLEDGEMENT

Thank you to all those who have encouraged me on my journey with Sam! Life often presents us with challenges and just like Sam, we all need our friends to walk alongside us to support and encourage.

I am especially indebted to my brothers and sisters at Beacon Church, to James and Lena who I met while spending time on Iona and to anyone else who enjoys these stories and passes them on.
Thanks too to Martin for his patience and excellent technical support.

These books are written with the help of my best friend, Jesus. They are his stories with the aim of teaching all who read them about the love and purpose he has for them. Please share them so that many more will be brought into his kingdom!

ABOUT THE AUTHOR

Gill Parkes

Gill lives in Norfolk with her husband where she enjoys walks along the beach and exploring the countryside. She loves to spend time with her grandchildren, especially snuggling up to share a good book.

Jesus is her best friend and she hopes that by reading these stories you will get to know him too.

PRAISE FOR AUTHOR

'Expertly written and full of scriptural knowledge and context, Gill Parkes has produced a valuable series of books for children that can be enjoyed by all ages and which skilfully and lovingly open up not just a world of exciting adventure but also the world of truth that is faith in Jesus Christ.'

- JAMES MACINTYRE
JOURNALIST AND AUTHOR

SAM PARROW'S TIME TRAVEL ADVENTURES

Sam travels through time to learn about God, how much he is loved and his own special place in God's world.

Sam Parrow And The Time Stone To Bethlehem

Sam Parrow Back In Time For Dinner

Sam Parrow And The Time Stone Secret

Sam Parrow Takes Time To Save A Dodo

Sam Parrow Back When Time Stood Still

Printed in Great Britain
by Amazon

78411159R00059